THIS BOOK BELONGS TO

. . . .

. . . .

I hope you enjoy this book and that it empowers you
to go out and achieve everything you've ever dreamed of doing.
In this book you will find all the lessons which I wish
I had learnt when I was younger.
As you go through your life, whatever happens,
I hope you always remember: I can, I will.

All my love, Esther

First published November 2019 by CPI Publishing
Revised second edition published May 2020 by CPI Publishing
This revised third edition published September 2020 by CPI Publishing

ISBN 978-1-8381612-1-7

SOPHIE SAYS
I CAN, I WILL

Join Sophie and Bunny on their journey,
as they learn that there is nothing that can
stop them from achieving their dreams!

ESTHER MARSHALL · BUZZ BURRY

One night Sophie lay wide awake in her bed,

with so many thoughts running through her head.

She dreamt about making
the world a better place,

so she got out her thinking hat,
and put on her game face.

"I can, I will," she said...

People would tell her certain jobs she could do,
but, quite rightly, she thought that could not be true.

She believed that whatever
she wanted, she'd be,

she'd achieve all she dreamed of;
just wait, you'll see.

"I can, I will," she said...

But Sophie just couldn't wait until the day,

she had to tell somebody, now, straight away.

So, she jumped out of bed, eyes open wide,
ran to her parents and began talking with pride.

"I can, I will," she said...

"I could be a teacher and work at a school,

I could help them learn
that education is cool.

Or maybe a doctor
or a nurse I could be,
finding cures for parents
and children like me."

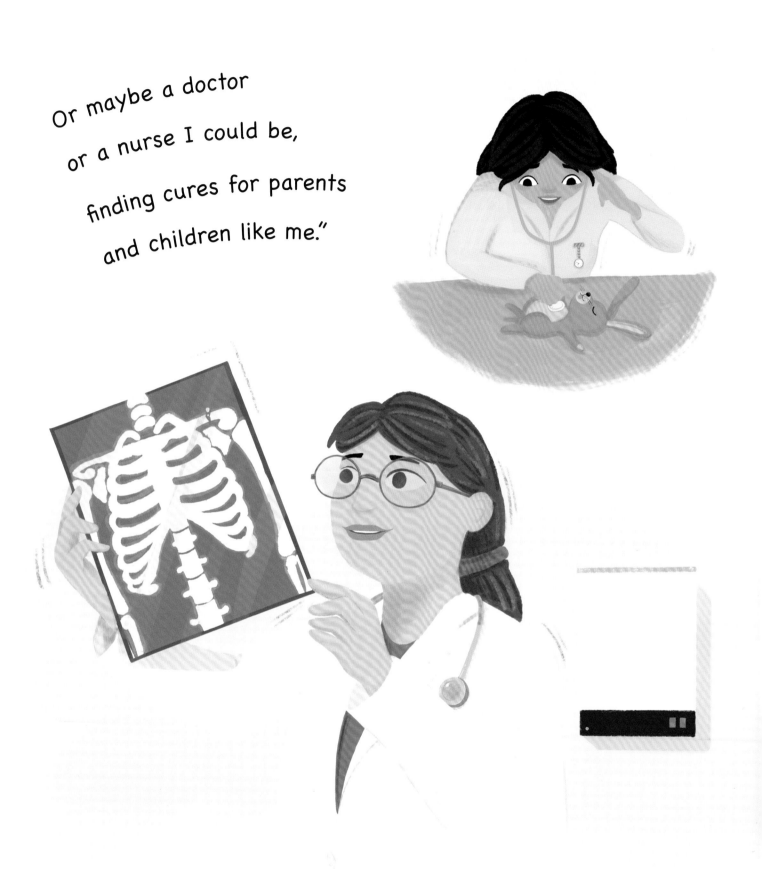

"I can, I will," she said...

"Or maybe in fact I could work on a plane,
as a pilot, or engineer, using my brain.

I would fly high in the sky up above,

soaring like an eagle in the clouds that I love."

"I can, I will," she said...

"Or I could work as a lawyer and go to the courts,

reading and writing important reports.

With a robe on my shoulders
and a wig on my hair,

I would fight to make
everything just,
right and fair."

"I can, I will," she said...

"I could be in the boardroom and head up a business,

taking on challenges, completely fearless.

Maybe science and technology could be for me, coding and experimenting to set the world free."

"I can, I will," she said...

"Or perhaps something in sport, representing my nation, winning medals and inspiring the next generation."

"I can, I will," she said...

When Sophie had finished all the thoughts in her head,
her parents both smiled, then looked at her and said:

"Come and sit with us, dear,
listen up, let's be clear."

"Whatever you do and whatever occurs, make sure people treat you with the respect you deserve.

Along the way people will tell you to stop,

But don't listen to them
and you'll rise to the top."

"Keep those who love you as your supportive team, believe in yourself and you will achieve your dreams."

"You can, you will," they said...

"And for those times when things don't go to plan,

when you're scared of failing,
remember you can!

You can do it!

Believe in
yourself!

You are great!

I can, I WILL!

Yipee!

Sometimes you'll make mistakes, and you might feel quite low,

but trust in yourself; see how far you can go!"

"Always keep kindness and love in your heart,
and you'll sure be off to a super, flying start."

"You can, you will,"
they said...

Sophie ran back upstairs
as her parents tucked her in bed,

they lent over and gave
her a big kiss on the head.

"But before you sleep, there's one last thing to say,

above all else be happy and you'll find your own way!"

"I can, I will," she said.